SOFIA MARTINEZ

Hector's Hiccups

by Jacqueline Jules

illustrated by Kim Smith

PICTURE WINDOW BOOKS

a capstone imprint

Sofia Martinez is published by
Picture Window Books, a Capstone Imprint
1710 Roe Crest Drive
North Mankato, MN 56003
www.mycapstone.com

Library of Congress Cataloging-in-Publication Data
Names: Jules, Jacqueline, 1956– author. | Smith, Kim,
1986– illustrator.

Title: Hector's hiccups / by Jacqueline Jules;
illustrated by Kim Smith.

Description: North Mankato, Minnesota : Picture
Window Books, a Capstone imprint, [2018] | Series:
Sofia Martinez | Includes Spanish words, a Spanish
glossary, discussion questions, and writing prompts.

Summary: Sofia's abuela is taking her and Sofia's
cousin Hector to the movies, but when Hector
develops hiccups, their movie plans are put on hold
until the children get their hiccup problem under
control.

Identifiers: LCCN 2017039786 (print) | LCCN
2017042406 (ebook) | ISBN 9781515823377 (eBook
PDF) | ISBN 9781515823353 (hardcover) | ISBN
9781515823414 (pbk.) Subjects: LCSH: Hiccups—
Juvenile fiction. | Hispanic American children—
Juvenile fiction. | Cousins—Juvenile fiction. |
Grandmothers--Juvenile fiction. | Hispanic American
families—Juvenile fiction. | CYAC: Hiccups—Fiction.
| Hispanic Americans—Fiction. |Cousins—Fiction. |
Grandmothers—Fiction. | Family life—Fiction.

Classification: LCC PZ7.J92947 (ebook) | LCC PZ7.
J92947 He 2018 (print) | DDC [E]—dc23

Designer: Aruna Rangarajan
Art Director: Kay Fraser

Printed and bound in the United States of America.
010838S18

TABLE OF CONTENTS

CHAPTER 1

HIC!

Movie day was finally here! Abuela was taking Sofia and her cousin Hector. They were going to see the movie *Jeffrey's Giant*.

They were all ready to go when they heard a loud noise.

"HIC! HIC!"

"What was that?" Abuela asked.

"HIC!"

"I think it was Hector," Sofia said.

"*HIC! HIC!*"

"Oh no! Hector has the hiccups!" Sofia said.

"*HIC! HIC!*" Hector replied.

"We should take care of this before the movie," Abuela said.

Abuela cut a slice of lemon. She gave it to Hector.

"This is what my abuela used to cure hiccups," she said.

It didn't work.

"*HIC! HIC!*"

"What about a glass of water?" Sofia said.

"Sí," Abuela agreed. "¡Agua!"

She gave Hector a glass. He took a big gulp.

"*HIC! HIC!*"

Water didn't work either.

"Nothing works! *HIC!*" Hector said. "I'm going to have the hiccups forever! *HIC! HIC!*"

"Just relax," Abuela said.

"Don't give up," Sofia said. "Try to hold your breath. I'll do it too."

Sofia and Hector held their breath together.

"Uno, dos, tres, cuatro, cinco . . ." Abuela counted.

After she reached ten, Abuela waved her arms. Then she shouted, "BOO!"

"*HIC! HIC!*"

Hector still had the hiccups.

"*HIC! HIC!*"

And now Sofia did too.

CHAPTER 2
Popcorn

"¡Ay dios mío!" Abuela said.

"Now I have two children with

hiccups."

"*HIC!*" Sofia answered.

"*HIC!*" Hector chimed in.

"Maybe we should watch a

movie at home," Abuela said.

"*HIC!* What about popcorn?"

Sofia asked.

"I love popcorn!" Hector said.

"We can make it ourselves,"

Abuela said.

Abuela took out a big pot. She poured a little oil in the bottom. She put in three kernels of popcorn.

"Why only three?" Sofia asked. "Do we each only get one piece of popcorn?"

Abuela laughed. "The first three kernels are a test. That's how we know when the oil is hot enough to cook the rest."

She put a lid on the pot. Then they waited.

Sofia hiccupped twice. *"HIC! HIC!"*

Then it was Hector's turn. *"HIC! HIC! HIC!"*

A few minutes later, they heard another sound. *POP! POP! POP!*

Abuela poured in more kernels. That's when it got very noisy.

POP! POP! HIC! POP! POP! POP! HIC! HIC!

"It's like music!" Abuela raised her arms. "¡Vamos a bailar!"

Sofia and Hector danced too.

POP! POP! POP! HIC! POP! HIC!

POP! POP! POP!

When the popcorn was ready,

Abuela poured it into a bowl.

She added salt and butter.

"¡Delicioso!" Sofia said.

It was still noisy, but not with

the same noise.

CRUNCH! CRUNCH! CRUNCH!

There were no more *POPS* or *HICS*!

"Yay!" Sofia cheered. "No more hiccups! Now we can go and see the movie."

Abuela looked at her watch. "We'll have to hurry."

CHAPTER 3

The Movie

The movie theater was not far, but there was a lot of traffic.

"Hurry, Abuela!" Sofia said.

"I'm going as fast as I can, sweet girl!" Abuela said.

When they got to the movie theater they had another problem.

"No parking spaces!" Hector said. "Now what?"

"Now we stay patient and calm and look for an open parking spot," Abuela said. "It's no use getting worked up."

"I am so excited for the movie! It's hard to wait," Hector said.

Abuela drove around the parking lot once. Then she drove around again. They finally found a spot in the very back.

"Hold my hands," Abuela said. "We'll run. Vámonos!"

They were all out of breath

when they bought their tickets. But

they had five minutes to spare!

Abuela stopped and bought popcorn and drinks.

"But we already had popcorn," Hector said.

"You can never have too much popcorn," Abuela said with a smile.

"I agree!" Sofia said.

Sofia, Abuela, and Hector settled in their seats. The lights went down and the music started.

"*HIC! HIC!*"

"Who was that?" Sofia asked.

"It wasn't me!" Hector said.

"HIC!"

It was **Abuela**!

"Ay dios mío!" she covered

her mouth. Sofia and Hector just

laughed.

Spanish Glossary

abuela — grandma

agua — water

ay dios mío — oh my goodness

delicioso — delicious

sí — yes

uno, dos, tres, cuatro, cinco — one, two, three, four, five

vámonos — let's go

vamos a bailar — let's dance

Talk It Out

1. What are some of the hiccup cures Sofia and her grandma used? What is your favorite hiccup cure?

2. Talk about a time you took a frustrating situation and made it better. What did you do?

3. Were you surprised by the ending of the story? Explain your answer.

Write It Down

1. Write the steps to making popcorn. Use the text on page 15 as your guide. Be sure to include all the ingredients and utensils needed.

2. Pretend you are Sofia. Write a journal entry about your day.

3. Pick your three favorite Spanish words or phrases from the story. Write three sentences using what you learned.

About the Author

Jacqueline Jules is the award-winning author of more than forty children's books, including *No English* (2012 Forward National Literature Award), *Zapato Power: Freddie Ramos Takes Off* (2010 CYBILS Literary Award, Maryland Blue Crab Young Reader Honor Award, and ALSC Great Early Elementary Reads), and *Freddie Ramos Makes a Splash* (named on 2013 List of Best Children's Books of the Year by Bank Street College Committee).

When not reading, writing, or teaching, Jacqueline enjoys time with her family in Northern Virginia.

About the Illustrator

Kim Smith has worked in magazines, advertising, animation, and children's gaming. She studied illustration at the Alberta College of Art and Design in Calgary, Alberta.

Kim is the illustrator of the upcoming middle-grade mystery series *The Ghost and Max Monroe*, the picture book *Over the River and Through the Woods*, and the cover of the forthcoming middle-grade novel *How to Make a Million*. She resides in Calgary, Alberta.

FUN
doesn't stop here!

- Videos & Contests
- Games & Puzzles
- Friends & Favorites
- Authors & Illustrators

Discover more at
www.capstonekids.com

See you soon!
¡Nos Vemos pronto!